TRANS FORMERS
ANIMATED
BE THE HERO

First published in the UK by HarperCollins Children's Books in 2009

1 3 5 7 9 10 8 6 4 2

ISBN 13: 978-0-00-729891-4

A CIP catalogue record for this title is available from the British Library.
www.harpercollins.co.uk

Quest for the Allspark

by Colin Brake

HarperCollins *Children's Books*

It has been another beautiful day in Detroit City but it's beginning to get dark now.

You're just finishing baseball practice. You've recently moved here and haven't yet made that many friends in your new neighbourhood but one girl you've met that has been friendly is Sari Sumdac. She's an interesting girl – full of wild ideas but she's also a bit of a loner. The kids at the baseball club you've joined say she's friends with the Autobots – the famous robot heroes. Maybe if you become friends with Sari she'll introduce you one day – that would be cool.

As you walk off the practice field you spot Sari sitting on a low wall, looking miserable. Her normally cheerful face is tense and it looks as if she might have been crying.

If you go across to speak to Sari, turn to 16

If you decide not to intrude, turn to 46.

You hesitate, not sure if you should go with Sari.

'It might be dangerous,' you explain.

'Of course it might,' she replies with a wild grin, 'but the Autobots could need us. We can't just ignore them. Come on,' she implores you.

'Okay,' you say, deciding that the adventure is worth pursuing. 'So where do we start?'

She tells you that the Autobots have a base in an abandoned motor plant in the old industrial sector of Detroit. 'My dad actually owns the place' she tells you, 'but I think he's forgotten about it.'

You travel across town on the subway and emerge from a station into the empty dark streets which used to house the beating heart of the American motor industry. These days it is full of empty buildings, boarded up and forgotten.

If Sari disappears, turn to 33.

If you think you can see something following you, turn to 51.

You tap Sari on the shoulder. 'How are we going to get to LA?' you ask.

Sari turns to you. 'Don't you know how fast Bumblebee is?'

Bumblebee changes into his vehicle form and races around the room before skidding to a halt and popping open his doors for you.

'Hold on tight,' he tells you and then sets off.

For you and Sari inside Bumblebee's comfortable seats, strapped in for safety, it is an exciting and exhilarating experience. For Bumblebee it is just pure fun. He loves to spin his wheels and due to his advanced Autobot construction he is able to do the journey in a couple of hours.

'But how will we find Bulkhead?' you ask.

'How about checking that out?' suggests Bumblebee pointing.

If he is pointing to a plume of black smoke, turn to 32.

If he is pointing to a huge fountain of flames, turn to 6.

4

The mysterious rod spins through the air and, as if in slow motion, Bumblebee leaps after it, arm outstretched and makes the catch.

'Oh yes,' shouts the hot-headed Autobot, 'and he's out!'

Bumblebee snaps the rod in two and then blasts each part with an energy bolt. The device emits a shower of blue sparks and then melts.

'Hey, he doesn't look like Prime anymore,' exclaims Bulkhead, who then nearly takes the stranger's head off with a massive double fisted punch.

'That's for playing with my sensors, pal,' he tells the stranger. The robot falls to the floor, totally deactivated.

You and Sari exchange a grin and high-five each other. 'Looks like we were right about that rod,' you tell her.

She nods. 'I guess it sent some kind of false signal into the Autobot's sensors,' she says.

Bulkhead and Bumblebee join you. 'Thanks for your help, kids,' says Bumblebee.

'Yeah,' adds Bulkhead sheepishly, 'without your help we'd still be fighting each other.'

Bumblebee takes a closer look at the deactivated

gardening 'bot. 'Decepticon circuitry,' he announces, 'looks like this guy had a Megatron-style upgrade.'

Bulkhead looks a bit embarrassed. 'I didn't mean to deactivate it,' he tells you.

'Don't worry,' Sari reassures him, 'once Megatron had him in his control he was as good as deactivated anyway.'

'What about the Allspark?' you ask suddenly, 'Megatron might have some other agents on the case.'

Bulkhead nods. 'This location is compromised anyway. I'll go and get my box.'

He disappears into the ruins of the still smoking building and emerges a few minutes later carrying a large box.

'Hadn't we better check whether it's the real Allspark or not?' you ask. The others agree.

If the box contains the Allspark, turn to 10.

If it contains a fake, turn to 50.

'Bulkhead must be here somewhere,' you point out to Sari, Bumblebee and Prowl, 'remember the gates?'

'Unless that was you, Prowl?' Sari wonders.

Prowl frowns. 'It is not my way to make an entrance like that. Your logic is right: our team-mate must be around here somewhere.'

Sari has a thought. 'Maybe he's inside the force-field?'

'Bulkhead can't generate a force-field,' Bumblebee tells you, 'not unless Ratchet gave him an upgrade when no-one was looking.'

'Bulkhead can't,' Sari agrees, 'but I bet the Allspark can.'

She pulls out the Key that hangs round her neck. 'And if the Allspark made that force-field I bet my Key can open it up again.'

'Follow me,' orders Prowl, 'and move carefully. That includes you, Bumblebee!'

When you reach the force-field Sari plunges her Key into the invisible wall.

If the wall becomes visible, turn to 90.

If Sari drops the Key, turn to 96.

A short distance away you can see a huge column of fire coming out of a building. Five giant fire engine 'bots are there, directing jets of water at the flames. You pull up opposite and Bumblebee lets you out and then changes. He asks the Fire Chief what's going on.

'Something wrong with your visual receptors pal?' he responds, without turning around, 'it's a fire!'

'I can see that,' Bumblebee replies with a good deal of patience, 'but what caused it?'

For the first time the Fire Chief takes a proper look at Bumblebee and his mouth drops open.

'You're... the hero 'bot, Bumblebee!' he gasps.

'Yeah, I know,' replies Bumblebee, 'but what I don't know is what started that blaze.'

'Take a look for yourself,' suggests the Fire Chief.

If Bulkhead appears out of the flames, turn to 53.

If Bumblebee goes into the burning building, turn to 25.

'Sari!' you call out, hopefully, 'Sari where are you?'

Sari suddenly rattles the chain-link fence that is running alongside the sidewalk and you realise that she's on the other side of it! 'There's a gap in the fence,' she tells you, 'come on!'

You find the gap and squeeze through into the grounds of a large disused motor factory.

'Is this it?' you ask her.

She nods and puts a finger to her lips. She leads you towards a side door.

'Why so quiet?' you whisper, 'I thought the Autobots were your friends.'

'They are,' replies Sari, just as quietly, 'but there might be Decepticons here too.'

The possibility of there being hostile forces around makes you shiver with fear. You look around, trying to see if you can spot any movement.

If you think you can see a vehicle parked in the street, turn to 48.

If you think you can see a man, turn to 12.

You hear the sound of something crashing around inside the park.

Bumblebee looks at you and Sari. 'I think you'd better stay here,' he tells you.

He disappears into the darkness.

You and Sari exchange looks.

'He might need our help,' says Sari.

You agree. 'But he told us to wait here,' you point out.

Sari grins. 'Does Bumblebee ever do what Prime tells him to do?' she asks, leading you into the park.

Inside it is very dark and frightening. The path leads you between very large works of art which tower menacingly above the walkway, as if they are about to fall on to you.

Suddenly the silence is shattered as something is hurled at great force through the air towards you. A 'bot crashes into the ground in front of you.

If it is Bumblebee, turn to 104.

If it is not Bumblebee, turn to 23.

'No,' you tell Sari, 'other way round; I'll go to Bumblebee, you handle the big one.'

Sari rolls her eyes. 'If you insist!' she mutters. She runs over to Bulkhead.

'Bulkhead, don't listen to him, that's not Prime,' she says.

Meanwhile you have run across to where the ex-gardening robot is helping Bumblebee to his feet. You see that he is holding a rod in his hand that is glowing blue. The rod has some buttons and other controls on it.

'You want me to stop Bulkhead?' Bumblebee is asking the stranger in confusion.

'Bumblebee, it's a trick. Don't do it,' you cry out, running between them.

The ex-gardening robot turns on you, his eyes burning with anger.

'Keep out of this human,' he growls at you fiercely. Bumblebee looks at him in amazement.

If Bulkhead hits the stranger, turn to 22.

If Bumblebee blasts at the stranger, turn to 49.

The box that Bulkhead is holding does contain the Allspark.

Suddenly there is a blur of action and three large vehicles pull up and change. It is Ratchet, Prowl and Optimus Prime.

'Well done, Autobots,' announces Prime. 'Our trick to uncover Megatron's latest plan has worked. Now we can make sure the plans for that device are destroyed.'

'And I'll give you all a little software patch to make sure no-one can use anything like that on us again,' adds Ratchet. 'Can't have us fighting amongst ourselves, can we?'

'What about the Allspark?' you wonder.

Optimus Prime tells you that it is probably best kept close to home. 'Talking of which it's time we all went home,' he tells you.

'Thanks for your help,' Bumblebee tells you. 'You were pretty awesome – for a human!'

The Autobots all laugh and you join in.

YOUR ADVENTURE WITH THE TRANSFORMERS IS OVER

'Yes,' Sari tells you firmly, 'anyway, it's not exactly the best district in town. It'll be much nicer having some company. Come on.'

She starts to head off in the direction of the nearest subway station. Half an hour later, when you reach the end of your journey on the subway, you see what she meant.

You emerge from the station into a desolate and forgotten part of the city. This is the heart of the old Motor City where, back in the twentieth century, America's car manufacturing industries were based.

Sari leads you across an empty lot, over rubble that might once have been a mall, towards a disused factory.

She heads to a small door at the side of the building and unlocks it.

She gestures for you to go inside.

If you go in first, turn to 59

If you want Sari to go first, turn to 75

You think you can see a man walking along the street but suddenly the figure changes into a vehicle and roars towards you. You call Sari but she's already turned back.

'Bumblebee!' she exclaims as the bright yellow vehicle screeches to a halt.

'Get in,' he tells you, flinging open his door. Sari pushes you inside and the door slams.

For a moment you wonder if you've done the right thing. The car speeds off as Bumblebee explains what is going on.

'Sorry to scare you, Sari,' he tells you. 'Who's your friend?' Sari introduces you and tells Bumblebee that you came with her to look for the Autobots. 'Good,' replies Bumblebee, 'we need all the help we can get.'

Sari asks why they didn't go into the Autobot's base. Bumblebee explains that the base is no longer safe; somehow Megatron has managed to gain control over the all the electrics at the old car plant. 'It's like Megatron's building now. Ratchet's working on a device to throw Megatron off line and take back what's ours,' he continues, 'but it's going to take time. In the meantime we're homeless.'

A worrying thought strikes Sari. 'What about the

Allspark?' she asks. The Allspark is the mystical source of all Autobot life and Megatron's ultimate goal is to control it.

Bumblebee tells you that Optimus Prime came up with a scheme to move the Allspark to a safe location; each of the Autobots took a box containing a replica of the Allspark to hide in a different location. 'One of the boxes had the real Allspark but none of us knew which,' he says. 'Trouble is the others never turned up at our meeting point and now I'm worried.'

If you have an idea, turn to 83.

If Sari suggests what to do, turn to 92.

'We need to have an idea of how big this force-field is,' you suggest.

Bumblebee points out that when he bounced off the wall it became visible for a split second. 'If we throw sticks at it,' he proposes, 'then it might light up and we can see how far it goes.'

Prowl agrees and leads you all, carefully, back to the point at which he was ejected by the force-field. He uses a handful of sticks gathered from the ground to test the space in front of you. When a stick hits the force-field it lights up briefly.

Sari reaches for the Key that she wears around her neck. 'Maybe my Key can open this,' she wonders. Without waiting for an answer she plunges the Key into the invisible wall.

If the wall becomes visible, turn to 90.

If Sari drops the Key, turn to 96.

14

Bulkhead gets between Bumblebee and the Professor's device. Bumblebee raises his hands ready to fire an energy blast but suddenly jerks his arms to one side and fires in another direction. The energy bolt hits a mirrored wall and bounces back.

'I knew all those hours playing pool would pay off!' shouts Bumblebee, as his energy blast smashes into the Professor's machine destroying it completely. Immediately Bulkhead staggers and rubs his head.

'Bumblebee!' he calls out.

'Now you know me?' asks Bumblebee.

'Of course I do,' replies the giant destruction 'bot.

'Well, you didn't a moment ago,' Bumblebee tells him.

'That machine of the Professor's must have been messing with your sensors, Bulkhead,' you tell him.

'Where is he anyway?' wonders Sari.

You look around and see the Professor running off in the distance.

'Don't worry,' says Bumblebee, changing to his vehicle form, 'he can't outrun me.'

Meanwhile Bulkhead is coming to terms with what he has done. He is looking at the wreckage of the building. 'Did I do that?'

'Don't worry,' Sari tells him, 'You were being duped by that machine. It made you think you were being attacked.'

'What about the Allspark?' you ask, remembering the main mission.

'It's hidden in there,' Bulkhead tells you, pointing towards the almost completely destroyed building. 'I'll go and get it.'

While Bulkhead goes to retrieve his box, Bumblebee returns with the captive Professor. He explains that he was given help by a mysterious online scientist to invent the Autobot-confusing device. 'Who helped you?' asks Sari.

The Professor shrugs. 'Some woman called Tron,' he tells you, 'Meg A. Tron.'

Bulkhead returns with his box. 'Better check it,' he suggests.

If the box contains the Allspark, turn to 10.

If it contains a fake, turn to 50.

The suction force from the street cleaning robot is incredible. You feel yourself being pulled by invisible hands towards the end of the dark tube, which looks like a nightmare snake above your head.

'Run! Get help!' you shout at Sari, who is rooted to the spot with fear.

You reach out and grab hold of a lamppost. The suction keeps increasing and you hold on desperately.

Your legs are now pointing almost straight up into the air and your feet are inside the mouth of the tube.

You feel your grip beginning to give way. You can't hold on any longer.

Suddenly there is a blur of movement down the street. Another vehicle is rushing towards you. It screeches to a halt and begins to change to robot mode...

If you think it is an Autobot, turn to 39.

If you think it is a Decepticon, turn to 62.

You walk across to where Sari is sitting, looking pretty glum. She doesn't see you approach so you clear your throat gently to get her attention. She turns quickly and you realise that you might have scared her.

'I'm sorry,' you blurt out, 'I didn't mean to make you jump.'

'That's alright,' she replies, 'I was miles away.'

'Something bothering you?' you ask gently.

'Is it that obvious?' she asks you back, managing to smile.

You nod and sit down next to her on the wall.

For a moment the pair of you just sit there in silence but eventually you can contain your curiosity no longer.

'Is it something to do with the Autobots?' you wonder and from Sari's expression it is clear that you've hit the nail on the head.

If Sari nods, turn to 26.

If she starts to cry and runs off, turn to 61.

Bumblebee and Sari take you inside the Autobots' base to make sure you are feeling better. You notice that Bumblebee is quite nervous and assure him that you are really okay now.

'It's not just you that I'm worried about,' he confesses.

'What's going on?' Sari asks him. 'Why did that cleaning robot attack us?'

Bumblebee shrugs. 'Isn't it obvious? It was Megatron making that machine attack you!'

You and Sari jump to your feet. 'Megatron?! The Autobots's deadliest enemy?'

'You know any other Megatron?' Bumblebee asks you.

Bumblebee explains that Megatron has discovered a way to control the City Authority robot force and has used this new power to launch an attack on the Autobots.

'He must be after the Allspark,' Sari guesses.

Bumblebee nods. 'Of course he is.'

'What is the Allspark?' You ask.

'It's the source of life for all 'bots,' Bumblebee tells you, 'and that's why Prime came up with a plan to hide it until the danger had passed.'

'So where have you hidden it?' you wonder.

Bumblebee spins around grinning. 'I don't know. No-one knows!'

Sari is confused. 'Someone must know,' she points out. 'Someone had to hide it.'

Bumblebee explains. 'Prime and Ratchet came up with a great plan. We got five identical boxes and put the Allspark in one of them. We put a fake Allspark in each of the others. Then we each took a box at random and took off to hide them in different locations. The idea is that none of us knew whether we had the real Allspark or not! But we were all meant to meet up here and no-one's turned up. Now I don't know what to do next.'

If Sari has an idea, turn to 54.

If you have an idea, turn to 21

18

You turn and look at Sari, shaking your head.

'Sorry Sari,' you tell her, 'but I can't argue with the science, can I?'

The Professor beams and takes a step towards Bulkhead. 'Now destroy that fake!' he orders.

'NO!!' Sari screams.

The Professor's hands are running over the device that is hanging around his neck. Why is he operating the machine now if it is just a scanner? The only answer is that the equipment does something else. You realise that you've been tricked and leap forward. You grab the device with both hands and pull hard. The strap snaps under the strain and you fall backwards, still holding the Professor's machine.

You let yourself fall and roll over.

'Bumblebee, zap it!' you call out.

If Bumblebee manages to fire at the machine, turn to 40.

If Bulkhead gets in the way, turn to 14.

You and Sari stop suddenly. In front of you is the clearance 'bot Crush-A and he has one of the Allspark boxes.

Suddenly an energy blast knocks it out of his grasp and, in a blur of speed, Bumblebee roars up and catches it.

'Bumblebee?' Sari exclaims, 'how did you get in?'

Bumblebee grins. 'With a little help from my friends.'

He throws the box into the air, as Crush-A tries to grab it from him.

Optimus Prime appears and makes a great catch. Ratchet, Prowl and Bulkhead are all with him.

They attack together but Crush-A fights back with incredible strength. The Autobots look to be in trouble.

'We need to help them,' says Sari.

You look at the battle raging in front of you and wonder what you can possibly do.

If you have an idea, turn to 44.

If Sari has an idea, turn to 63.

Sari shakes her head firmly. 'No way' she tells you, 'how could anyone fake that?'

You shrug. 'Come on Sari, you can do anything with computer graphics these days, if you've got enough processing power.'

'Oh, no!' shrieks Sari. 'Maybe you're right.'

'There's only one way to find out for sure,' you tell her, 'we'll have to go and look for the Autobots – the real Autobots – and make sure they're okay.'

Sari nods in agreement. 'We'll go and take a look at their base for a start. Whoever did send that message didn't want me to go anywhere near it which is a good reason to start there, if you ask me!'

'What do you mean – we'll go?' you ask Sari

'Aren't you coming with me?' she replies with a grin.

If you agree to go with Sari, turn to 38.

If you hesitate, turn to 2.

'Don't you have any communications equipment in here?' you ask, looking around at the Autobots' base.

'Yes, but the system's been down,' Bumblebee explains. 'I guess it's worth having another go.'

He runs across to a console near to one of the large screens and operates some switches.

'Looks like there's still some interference out there,' he tells you.

'Do you think it might be Megatron?' Sari wonders.

'Either that or Prime forgot to pay the 'phone bill,' Bumblebee jokes. He jabs a finger into one of the inputs on the console and fires a controlled blast of energy into the system.

'That should boost the signal,' he says and the screen flickers into life.

At first it is a mess of static but then the picture stabilises and you can just about make out an Autobot.

If it is Ratchet, turn to 80.

If it is Prowl, turn to 30.

22

Bulkhead swings his demolition ball and knocks the stranger off his feet. The big demolition robot then starts hitting him with his pile driver fists.

The stranger is strong though and starts to duck and weave to avoid the blows.

'Come on, Bumblebee,' shouts Bulkhead, 'join in any time.'

Bumblebee is still not sure. 'But it's Prime,' he tells his friend.

Bulkhead swings another punch at the impostor but fails to connect.

'It might look like Prime but it isn't him,' insists Bulkhead, 'Prime would never talk to Sari or one of her human friends like that.'

You can see that Bulkhead is getting through to Bumblebee. The stranger presses a button on his control rod and it glows stronger.

'Bulkhead – the rod!' you shout.

Bulkhead knocks the rod out of the stranger's hand.

If Bumblebee catches it, turn to 4.

If it falls on the floor, turn to 56.

'Prowl!' screams Sari as she recognises the crumpled form before you.

Prowl gathers himself up and, in one smooth and apparently effortless movement, he gets to his feet. 'Please do not shout, Sari,' he asks politely, 'my audio circuits are functioning at normal capacity.'

Prowl tells you that there is a force-field surrounding some of the works of art. 'When I tried to pass through it ejected me.'

'Guess you just weren't fast enough,' says Bumblebee, dashing off to have a go himself.

Moments later he is flung backwards as if he has run into a bouncy castle.

'Wheee!' calls Bumblebee as he flies through the air, 'this is fun!'

He hits a tree and slides to the ground. 'Apart from that bit,' he tells you.

If you suggest trying to find out how big the force-field is, turn to 13.

If you decide to try and find Bulkhead, turn to 5.

The speaker is another 'bot. It looks like a gardening robot but it suddenly begins to change into...

'Prime!?' Bumblebee calls out in surprise, raising his head and looking over in confusion. 'What are you doing here?'

Bumblebee tries to pull himself up.

The gardening 'bot runs across and starts to help Bumblebee. 'Something's fried Bulkhead's circuits,' he tells him urgently, 'we have to take him down before he destroys the whole city.'

You and Sari look at each other in amazement.

'Why are they calling that thing Prime?' you ask.

'I don't know,' Sari replies, 'It must be some kind of illusion only 'bots can see.'

'We have to do something,' you insist, 'or the hero 'bots are going to destroy themselves.'

Sari nods. 'They'll never harm a human, not deliberately. You take Bulkhead and I'll deal with Bumblebee. Agreed?'

If you agree, turn to 43.

If you disagree, turn to 9.

As you and Sari watch in horror Bumblebee darts forward to go into the burning building but the heat is too great for him. 'It's no good,' he tells you, 'I've got to put the fire out first.'

He asks the Fire Engine 'bots to move back from the building and then starts driving. He quickly builds up speed, racing around and around the building, building up an incredible vacuum that deprives the fire of oxygen. Suddenly the fire just dies - as if someone had switched it off, which is exactly what Bumblebee has done.

Bumblebee slows down, changes into robot mode and heads into the now smoking remains of the building. But before he can get inside, a wrecking ball swings out and knocks him to the ground.

Sari runs up to check that he is alright.

'Keep back,' Bumblebee warns her, jumping back on to his feet.

Bulkhead appears in the doorway to the building and immediately punches out with one of his battering ram arms. Bumblebee uses his speed to duck out of the way of the blow but is then caught by Bulkhead's other arm following through. Bumblebee sails through the air like a rag doll and into a nearby skyscraper. He slides down the wall and lands in a crumpled heap.

'Bulkhead! What are you doing?' screams Sari.

'Is that you Sari?' rumbles Bulkhead.

'Yes it is. And that's Bumblebee that you've just knocked into next week,' she tells him.

'No it's not,' replies Bulkhead, 'that's an imposter. That's not the real Bumblebee.'

'How do you make that out?' you ask the massive demolition 'bot.

'I told him,' says a new voice.

If the speaker is another human, turn to 73.

If the speaker is another robot, turn to 24.

Sari looks up and wipes her face.

'I haven't seen the Autobots for days,' she tells you. 'No-one has.'

You realise that she's right; there's been nothing on the news channels for days about Detroit's very own robotic superheroes.

'Maybe they're off somewhere on a mission,' you suggest.

Sari shakes her head. 'Bumblebee would have told me,' she insists.

'Well, there's no point worrying,' you tell Sari, 'why don't you look for them? Do they have a home?'

Sari nods. 'I called but there was no reply.' She gets to her feet. 'You're right though; that's where I should start looking for them.'

She begins to walk away but stops and looks back at you.

'Are you coming or what?' she demands.

You just look at her.

'Well, it was your idea,' she tells you, grinning.

If you go with Sari, turn to 74.

If you're not sure, turn to 47.

27

Standing before you is Optimus Prime. He has a box like the others you have seen – a box for holding the Allspark or one of its fake doubles. Suddenly he flies backwards as he is grabbed by a giant clearance 'bot.

'The name's Crush-A, pal,' says the stranger slamming Prime into a wall, 'and I'm taking this whether you like it or not.' He grabs the box.

Suddenly the rest of the Autobots are there too; all joining the attack on Crush-A. Bumblebee fires energy bolts, Ratchet tries to unbalance him with his magnetism, Bulkhead pounds him with his pile driver arms and Prowl uses his martial arts fighting moves.

Incredibly the enemy 'bot stands firm. If anything he seems to get stronger the longer the fight goes on. It's obvious that the Autobots need your help.

If you have an idea, turn to 44.

If Sari has an idea, turn to 63.

The Library is a massive glass-fronted building formally a warehouse. When you arrive you find it dark and closed for business for the day. There is no immediate sign of Prime.

Prowl suggests that you split up to look for a way in. You, Sari and Bumblebee go around to the rear of the building. You spot an open window and Bumblebee helps you to reach it. You manage to squeeze through and Sari follows you but the opening is far too small for Bumblebee. You promise to find a door to unlock from inside to let the Autobots in.

Inside the Library it is dark and spooky. There are miles and miles of shelves full of books and your footsteps echo on the cold tiles.

Suddenly you hear a commotion from above.

If you met Crush-A earlier, turn to 19.

If you have not encountered Crush-A, turn to 27.

Sari begins running in the direction of the sound. 'It's the Autobots,' she cries out before disappearing into the darkness.

'Wait!' you call but she has already gone. You are worried that it might not be the Autobots at all.

Moving with more caution you continue heading in the direction that Sari took.

Eventually you enter into a large space that might once have been the main assembly line area of the factory. Now it is the living area of the Autobots. The engine sound you heard earlier is coming from somewhere in this location.

You strain your eyes but can't make out what it is.

You think about calling out Sari's name but don't want to draw attention to your position.

Suddenly something comes hurtling out of the darkness towards you.

If it is Sari, turn to 41.

If it is a robot, turn to 31.

The figure on the screen is Prowl. The communications link is clearly two-way as Prowl immediately points in your direction.

'Who's the other human?' he demands.

'A friend,' Sari and Bumblebee say together, and you find yourself blushing.

Prowl leans into the camera urgently.

'We need all the friends we can get,' he tells you.

Bumblebee steps forward. 'Have you heard from Prime?' he asks.

'No, I have had no contact with anyone since I began this mission.'

'Where are you?' asks Bumblebee.

'On my way back from Texas,' explains Prowl. 'And I know where Bulkhead was going. I suggest we meet there.'

Bumblebee nods and changes into his vehicle form. You and Sari get on board.

'So where are we heading?' Bumblebee asks.

If Prowl tells you to go to New York, turn to 55.

If Prowl tells you to go to Los Angeles, turn to 3.

Out of the darkness a robot vehicle appears, rumbling relentlessly towards you.

Bright headlights on the front of the machine half-blind you.

'Run!' cries Sari from somewhere off to the side.

For a moment you are transfixed. The machine is a bit like a vacuum cleaner 'bot but this model is much bigger than any domestic robot you've ever seen. This is an industrial scale machine, as big as a school bus.

A robot arm on top of the body of the machine controls a giant vacuum tube which sweeps through the air like an angry snake. You realise with a shock that the tube is heading for you. A terrific suction force pulls you into the air.

Suddenly another vehicle screeches to a halt and begins to change.

If you think it is an Autobot, turn to 39.

If you think it is a Decepticon, turn to 62.

There is a big black plume of smoke reaching into the sky.

'Some kind of blaze,' comments Bumblebee, 'what's the betting it's got something to do with Bulkhead?'

Bumblebee changes again and takes you and Sari to the site of the fire. It's a massive warehouse that is almost entirely consumed by flames. The local fire service is using four robot fire engines to pump huge jets of water into the flames, which is adding to the dense black smoke.

Sari finds a police officer and asks if he knows what happened.

'Some kind of robot fight,' he tells her, 'looks like it got a bit out of hand!'

Bumblebee grins. 'Definitely sounds like Bulkhead!'

'If your friend is in there, he'd better get out before the building collapses,' says the policeman.

If Bulkhead appears out of the flames, turn to 53.

If Bumblebee goes into the burning building, turn to 25.

Suddenly you realise that you cannot see Sari anymore. It is very dark in this neighbourhood; the streetlights don't all work and in the deep pools of darkness between the remaining lights it is difficult to see much at all.

'Sari?' you call out anxiously and for a long moment you hear nothing, save for the distant sounds of the modern city a few blocks to the North.

'It's okay,' Sari says suddenly, popping out from the concealed entrance to a nearby alley. 'This way,' she insists and heads back into the blackness of the tiny alleyway.

You begin to follow her, but as you step into the alley you cast a glance over your shoulder and think you see a movement. You stop, step back, and take another look.

If you think you can see a vehicle parked in the street, turn to 48.

If you think you can see a man, turn to 12.

Sari tells you that she is good at riddles.

'Go on then,' says Bumblebee, 'solve this one.'

'Well, black and white, that sounds like printing to me, like in a newspaper or a book,' explains Sari slowly, 'and newspapers and books are things that are "read" all over the city. So you see, it's a sort of play on words. "Read" meaning something that's been read rather than "red" the colour.'

Bulkhead and Bumblebee look at each other.

'I still don't get it,' rumbles Bulkhead.

'Me neither,' confesses Bumblebee, 'where do you go for books and newspapers? Lots of places!'

'But there's only one Central Library – and it's massive,' you point out. 'We were told at school that they take a copy of every paper and every book that comes out.'

If Prowl suggests a strategy, turn to 64.

If you go directly to the Library, turn to 28.

Prowl thinks that you should split up and approach the club separately. He suggests that you, Sari and Bumblebee go in the front of the club while he and Bulkhead enter from the rear.

The club is in downtown Detroit. When you arrive you find that it is closed – a notice on the door tells customers that it is being refurbished. Bumblebee tries the front door and finds that it is slightly open.

'Hey, what do you know?' he announces, 'the Jam Jar door is ajar!'

He pushes the door open and you slip inside. You find yourselves in an impressive foyer area.

Suddenly you hear something thudding loudly in another room.

'It's coming from in there,' says Sari pointing at double doors leading to the main performance area.

Without warning the doors fly open.

If you met Crush-A earlier, turn to 77.

If you have not encountered Crush-A, turn to 70.

'Show me what you mean?' you ask the Professor.

He waves his hand at the read-outs on the device that is hanging around his neck like the boxes of nuts at a football game.

'The Autobot heroes are all from another world,' he reminds you, 'but these read-outs show us that this so-called Bumblebee was made right here in the United States.'

'Probably by Megatron,' rumbles Bulkhead.

Sari looks at you, shocked.

'What are you doing?' she demands. 'You're not actually listening to that man are you?'

You point at the Professor's device. 'You can't argue with the science,' you tell Sari.

'But that is Bumblebee,' she insists, 'I know it is.'

You look at Sari and can see that she is really certain about this.

If you decide to believe Sari, turn to 66.

If you decide to believe the Professor, turn to 18.

Sari screams at you, 'Run!'

She turns and sprints and you do the same thing.

You run as fast as you can, your heart beating wildly.

You dare to look over your shoulder and see that the street cleaning robot has started to move much faster. It is chasing you and, more worryingly, it is catching up to you.

The suction tube of the powerful vacuum looms over your head and you can feel the tremendous force pulling you back and slowing you down.

You reach out and wrap your arms around a fire hydrant but the force is too great.

Sari has stopped to see what is happening to you. 'Hold on!' she screams. Another vehicle suddenly roars down the street. It skids to a halt and changes...

If you think it is an Autobot, turn to 39.

If you think it is a Decepticon, turn to 62.

Sari explains that the Autobots have a secret base in the old part of the city.

'The old industrial area?' you ask, knowing that it is an area dating back to the days when Detroit was the Motor City – the vibrant heart of America's automobile industry. Now the district is just derelict; the factories that were still standing are boarded up, empty and forgotten. Except for one.

'My Dad owned this old plant,' Sari tells you proudly, 'and it made a perfect base for the Autobots.'

A short subway ride later and you find yourself walking the dark streets, between the massive old abandoned factory buildings. It is a bit spooky and you look around you nervously. You think you see something moving and look again.

If you think you can see a vehicle parked in the street, turn to 48.

If you think you can see a man, turn to 12.

You see a flash of yellow and then something moving very fast whizzes around the cleaning robot firing electrical power blasts at it from all sides. The cleaning machine doesn't have a chance. It vibrates and shakes and comes to a grinding halt. The vacuum tube collapses and the suction power is turned off. You fall to the floor.

You look up into the faces of Sari and, above her, the Autobot hero, Bumblebee.

'Is your friend okay?' asks Bumblebee. 'I was trying to perform a rescue, not make things worse.'

You get to your feet and assure Bumblebee that you are fine.

'Better than that thing anyway,' you say pointing at the cleaning machine, which is still sparking with residual energy from Bumblebee's blasts.

If you were attacked on the street, turn to 17.

If you were attacked inside the factory, turn to 69.

Bumblebee fires at the machine but the Professor leaps forward and pulls it clear of the energy blast. Sari jumps on the Professor's back and forces him to let go of the device.

Bumblebee takes aim again and this time his energy bolt hits the machine square on. It explodes and as it is destroyed Bulkhead cries out and puts his hands to his head.

'Are you alright?' Sari asks him, anxiously.

'Yeah, fine now but I've got a major case of circuit ache,' Bulkhead replies.

'Do you still think I'm not me?' asks Bumblebee.

'Of course you're you,' says Bulkhead. You and Sari high-five each other.

'The professor's machine must have been making you see things that weren't there,' guesses Sari.

'Talking of the Professor – where did he go?' you ask, spinning around. You see him running off down the street.

Bumblebee changes into his vehicle form. 'Looks like a job for me,' he says and roars off at speed.

Bulkhead looks forlornly at the smoking building he nearly destroyed. 'I can't believe I did that,' he mutters.

'It wasn't your fault,' Sari reminds him.

'But I hid the Allspark in there,' Bulkhead realises suddenly, 'it's not going to be safe now, is it?'

Bulkhead goes back inside to collect the box he hid. Bumblebee draws up and you can see that he has the Professor inside. As police 'bots put him in handcuffs, the Professor confesses that the machine was designed with the help of a woman he met online. A woman with a peculiar surname – Tron. 'What was her first name?' you ask him.

'Meg,' he answers, 'Meg A. Tron.'

Bulkhead returns holding his secure box.

If the box contains the Allspark, turn to 10.

If it contains a fake, turn to 50.

Sari bundles into you, almost knocking you from your feet.

'It's not an Autobot,' she gasps.

Bright lights suddenly wash over you and you can see what it is that is chasing your friend.

It looks like a cleaning robot, but on a massive scale. Most households in robot-mad Detroit have cleaning robots but this is the size of a small van, built to clean industrial sites. Its headlights are pointing right at you as it rumbles quickly towards you.

From the top of the robot vehicle a massive suction tube on an arm reaches out like a giant tentacle towards you.

You experience a terrific force pulling you up. You grab hold of something but the suction is too strong.

Suddenly you hear another engine.

If you think it is an Autobot, turn to 39.

If you think it is a Decepticon, turn to 62.

'We're going to take you down!' Bumblebee tells Crush-A and, using his super speed, he snatches the box from out of the hands of the enemy robot.

'Go long,' calls Bumblebee and launches the box into the air like a ball. Bulkhead, reacting with unusual speed, moves into position and makes a great reception.

You see an exhibit entitled "Connections" which gives you an idea. It's just a pile of old-fashioned rope draped over a collection of odd shapes. You feel a bit bad about damaging a so-called work of art but Bumblebee needs your help,

'Hey, Bumblebee,' you shout out, 'could you use this?' You throw one end of the rope to Bumblebee who grabs it and rushes off at his top speed. All you can see is a yellow blur as if someone had smudged a painting. Suddenly Bumblebee comes to a halt and passes one end of the rope to Bulkhead. Crush-A looks down and sees that his entire lower body is now wrapped in a coil of rope. Bulkhead jerks his end of the rope backwards and Crush-A crashes to the floor.

Meanwhile Sari has moved over to the box that Bulkhead had been protecting. She opens the lid to check on the contents. 'This isn't the real Allspark,' she announces.

A split second later there is a flash of light and Crush-A disappears into thin air, leaving the coil of rope to fall to the ground empty.

A new 'bot arrives on the scene. It is the ninja-like Autobot Prowl.

'You're too late,' Bulkhead tells Prowl, 'we could have done with your help a few minutes ago!'

If you get a message from Ratchet, turn to 100.

If you get a message from Prime, turn to 78.

You nod and hurry across to the giant demolition 'bot, Bulkhead.

'You have to listen to me,' you yell at him, 'that's not the real Prime.'

Bulkhead swings his head to look at the stranger who is just helping Bumblebee to his feet.

'It looks like Prime,' he says in his deep, echoing voice.

'But it's an illusion!'

Sari is trying to tell Bumblebee the same thing. You see that the stranger 'bot is holding something in one of his hands; some sort of device with control buttons on it. It's glowing with a blue light. Is it possible that it is the source of the illusions?

You call out to Sari. 'Get the rod thing out of his hand!'

The stranger looks at you, with hatred in his eyes.

'Be silent, human.'

If Bulkhead hits the stranger, turn to 22.

If Bumblebee blasts the stranger, turn to 49.

You watch the fight carefully and think you can see something that might be important. 'He's getting stronger,' you tell Sari, 'as if he's absorbing the energy of everything we're throwing at him.'

Sari nods. 'Yes, you're right,' she agrees, 'but how does that help?'

You shrug. 'I don't know, maybe there's a limit to the energy he can store,' you speculate. 'You can't keep charging a battery once it is fully charged, can you?'

Bumblebee crashes into the wall close to where you are hiding.

'This guy just won't go down,' he mutters, as he gets to his feet.

You tell him your theory about Crush-A having a limit to the energy he can store. Bumblebee nods as you explain. 'Yeah, that makes sense,' he tells you. He reaches for a nearby electrical socket.

'Never do anything like this at home kids,' he tells you seriously, 'you should never play with electricity but my circuits are fully insulated so, with luck, I won't fry.'

With that he accesses the building's electrical supply and uses it to amplify his energy blast. A multicoloured wave of light hits Crush-A, who glows bright blue and then overloads in a burst of intense light. When your eyes recover you can see that he is lying defeated on the ground.

Ratchet examines the now non-functioning 'bot. 'Definite signs of Decepticon circuitry,' he tells you.

Bumblebee shakes his head. 'I can't believe we nearly handed an agent of Megatron the Allspark on a plate,' he says.

'We didn't,' grins Optimus Prime.

Bumblebee doesn't get the joke. 'What's so funny?'

'The Allspark was never in any danger!' Prime explains.

'All the boxes contained fakes,' adds Ratchet.

If you are in the Library, turn to 105.

If you are in the Night Club, turn to 103.

The Sculpture Park is an area of park and woodland with a number of paths through it leading visitors through a trail of different kinds of sculpture. There are some traditional-looking statues and some very modern sculptures made of all sorts of everyday things. It's a really interesting place to visit during the day but at night it is unlit and very spooky.

Bumblebee lets you and Sari climb out and then changes into his robot form.

'That's not right,' he says and points towards the massive iron gates that form the main entrance to the Park. They are wide open and when you look closer you can see that the lock on them has been broken.

'Something or someone with enormous strength did this,' suggests Sari, looking at the damage.

If Bumblebee leads the way into the park, turn to 86.

If you hear something inside the park, turn to 8.

You walk past Sari and head for the bus stop. As you pass her you hear a sob and decide that you can't just ignore her.

'Are you okay?' you ask her.

'Does it look like it?' she snaps back.

You raise your hands. 'Hey, no need to bite,' you tell her, 'I was just asking.'

Sari jumps up and steps towards you. 'I'm sorry,' she says and you can tell by her tone that she means it, 'I'm just a bit upset about something. I didn't mean to take it out on you.'

'Is it something to do with the Autobots?' you guess.

Sari nods. 'I got this message from them telling me to keep away,' she explains, 'but it doesn't make any sense.'

If Sari shows you the message, turn to 58.

If she tells you what the Autobots said, turn to 89.

You hesitate, not sure if you should go with Sari.

'Come on,' she says, 'if we find them you'll get to meet the Autobots.'

Your face lights up. Meeting the Autobots in person would be cool. Although some might be more fun than others.

'Is Ratchet really as moody as he looks?' you ask.

Sari laughs. 'A bit.'

Sari tells you that the location of the Autobots' base is a secret that you must promise to keep.

She takes you to old downtown Detroit, which is full of abandoned car factories dating back to the twentieth century. It's dark and spooky here, with no-one around. As you walk along the shadowy streets following Sari's lead you suddenly sense something moving just behind you.

You whirl around but the street is totally empty.

'Did you see something?' you stammer.

If she did, turn to 87.

If she didn't, turn to 98.

You think you can see a vehicle parked in the street but you are sure the street was empty a moment ago. You turn to call Sari and when you check back there is nothing there again. You frown. Suddenly there is an engine roar and the sound of fast spinning wheels. A bright yellow vehicle appears from a side street, roaring towards you. You think it is going to hit you but at the last moment it swerves, skids and comes to a halt right in front of you. The doors pop open and a friendly, excitable voice calls out to you.

'Get in!' Sari is grinning broadly and grabs you by the hand. 'Come on!' she urges you and bundles you into the car. The doors slam shut and the engine bursts back into life hurling you deep into the seats with the sudden acceleration.

'It's Bumblebee!' she tells you and introduces you to her Autobot friend.

'Hope I didn't make you jump out of your paint jobs there,' he tells you 'but I had to stop you going into the base.'

He explains that Megatron has found a way to take control of the base and that the Autobots have headed out to protect the Allspark - the source of all Autobot life.

Bumblebee tells you about the plan devised by Optimus Prime. Each Autobot took a box containing a replica of the Allspark to hide in a different location. 'But one of them was the genuine Allspark,' he adds.

'But none of you knew which one?' Sari guesses.

'Yeah,' Bumblebee tells her, 'but none of the other 'bots have made it back to the meeting point and I don't know what to do!'

If you have an idea, turn to 83.

If Sari suggests what to do, turn to 92.

Suddenly there is a blast of electric energy as a power bolt flashes out of Bumblebee's outstretched arms. The bolt of energy is aimed at the control rod, but the stranger sees the danger and manages to twist his body out of the way.

'Bulkhead – we need to get that thing out of his hands,' Bumblebee shouts across at the big demolition robot.

Bulkhead is still confused. 'But that's Prime,' he insists.

Bumblebee speeds around his friend. 'Come on Bulkhead, think about it. I wouldn't be fighting Optimus Prime like this, would I?'

You can almost hear the sound of Bulkhead's circuits whirring as considers this argument.

Meanwhile the stranger is busy reprogramming his control rod.

Bravely, you run and jump up at the stranger, managing to knock the device out of his hand.

If Bumblebee catches it, turn to 4.

If it falls on the floor, turn to 56.

The box contains a fake Allspark. You are all relieved.

'This thing came close but it wouldn't have got the real Allspark even if it had been successful,' you point out.

'But the real Allspark is still out there,' Bumblebee reminds you, 'and we don't know where the rest of the guys are.'

Another Autobot appears behind you. It is the mysterious Prowl, who moves quickly but silently like a panther.

'I am here,' announces Prowl. 'But I have no idea where Prime and Ratchet are,' he adds.

'Were you attacked?' Bumblebee asks Prowl.

Prowl shakes his head. 'My Allspark is safely hidden,' he tells you.

'We need to find the others,' you suggest, 'they might not have been as lucky as Prowl.'

'I guess the quest isn't over yet,' says Sari.

If you get a message from Ratchet, turn to 100.

If you get a message from Prime, turn to 78.

It is dark and mysterious in this part of the City. Few people live here and hardly anyone comes here to work anymore. There is just block after block of old factories and manufacturing plants, massive buildings that haven't been inhabited for over a hundred years. It feels like a place of ghosts, but not a classic haunted house. The ghosts here are the dead spirits of thousands of cars and the men and women who designed and made them.

You catch a glimpse of something out of the corner of your eye, something moving. Has one of your ghosts manifested itself for real?

You think about telling Sari but she is striding ahead.

You see the movement again and spin around, determined to catch whatever it is in the act.

If you think you can see a vehicle parked in the street, turn to 48.

If you think you can see a man, turn to 12.

Sari agrees with you. 'How could I have been so stupid?' she mutters, furious at being taken in so badly, 'it's obvious.'

'Don't beat yourself up over it,' you tell Sari, 'you know how clever computers are!'

Sari is thinking the situation through. 'So if that was a fake message I got, why did someone want me to stay away from the Autobots?'

'Maybe they wanted to keep something you've got away from the Autobots,' you suggest.

'My Key!' Sari exclaims, 'It's linked to the Allspark somehow and I can use it to heal the Autobots if they get damaged...'

'Or attacked?' you suggest.

You can see that Sari is really worried now. 'We need to go and find the Autobots,' she announces.

If Sari takes you to the Autobots base, turn to 94.

If she hesitates about taking you with her, turn to 81.

53

Suddenly a massive figure appears out of the flames. You recognise the familiar shape of the Autobot hero Bulkhead but before anyone can greet him the demolition 'bot swings his massive wrecking ball and knocks Bumblebee off his feet. You and Sari have to dive for cover as the ball hits a wall, sending bricks and other debris falling to the ground.

'Are you okay?' Sari calls to Bumblebee, but the speedster is already getting to his feet.

'Don't worry about me,' he calls out and changes into his vehicle form again.

Bulkhead advances on him, swinging his massive battering ram arms.

'If one of those connects,' you whisper to Sari, 'Bumblebee might fly back to Detroit faster than he got here!' Seconds later your prediction nearly comes true. One of Bulkhead's giant fists catches the underside of the racing Bumblebee and he flies into the air. Luckily he manages to change in mid-flight and, as he hurtles into a nearby skyscraper, he is able to steady himself. For a moment he is clinging to the tall building like a bug. Then Bulkhead hits him again with the wrecking ball and Bumblebee is dislodged. He hits the ground and the whole area shakes.

Bravely, Sari breaks cover and rushes in front of the marauding Bulkhead.

'What are you doing?' she demands.

'Get out of my way Sari. That isn't Bumblebee,' replies Bulkhead.

'What are you talking about?' Sari replies, holding her ground, 'Of course that's Bumblebee.'

Bulkhead shakes his massive head. 'No it's not. It's a trick. That's a fake Bumblebee.'

'Where did you get an idea like that?' you ask, joining Sari.

'From me,' says a new voice.

If the speaker is another human, turn to 73.

If the speaker is another robot, turn to 24.

Sari gets to her feet.

'Come on Bumblebee, don't just give up,' she tells him. She waves her hand at all the bits and pieces of equipment in the base. 'You've got all this technology – why don't you use it?'

Bumblebee gets to his feet and speeds across to the communications equipment.

'You're right,' he tells Sari, 'We've got to try and find them. Let's see if any of them are in communications range.'

He turns the equipment on but the screen fills with noisy static.

'That doesn't look right,' you comment.

Bumblebee agrees. 'Looks like Megatron is trying to jam our signals but I can boost the power...'

He jabs a finger into a socket on the side of the screen and loads some extra energy into the system.

The screen clears to reveal an Autobot.

If it is Ratchet, turn to 80.

If it is Prowl, turn to 30.

'How are we going to get to New York?' you ask.

Bumblebee laughs. 'Haven't you heard? I'm built for speed! Let's go!'

The journey seems to take no time at all. The world rushes past his windows in a blur and before you know it you are in New York City.

Bumblebee slows down as you drive over one of the many bridges that link Manhattan Island to the mainland.

'How are we going to find Bulkhead?' you ask. 'New York is a big city.'

You and Sari climb out of Bumblebee and he changes back into his robot form.

He looks around and then grins.

'How about over there?' he suggests, pointing to something in the distance. You turn around and look in the direction he is indicating.

If you see a plume of black smoke, turn to 32.

If you see a huge fountain of flames, turn to 6.

The mysterious rod spins and falls to the floor. For a moment nothing happens then Bumblebee and the stranger both leap for it. They fall into a mass of arms and legs, a whirling mass of 'bot, rolling over and over. Suddenly something glowing blue pops out and rolls to your feet.

You pick it up and throw it across to Bulkhead.

'Hey you!' roars Bulkhead. 'Looking for something?'

He holds up the rod. The two fighting 'bots stop instantly. Bulkhead calmly snaps the rod in two. 'Nooo!' cries out the stranger and jumps forwards to try and retrieve the bits.

'Oh, no, you don't,' says Bumblebee and fires a pair of energy blasts at the pieces, utterly destroying them.

The stranger stops and looks confused, as if he doesn't know quite what to do now.

Bulkhead makes up his mind for him and hits him with a massive fist. The stranger flies up into the air and comes down hard at Bumblebee's feet.

'And he's out!' he calls out, triumphantly.

You and Sari give each other a hug. 'We were right,' she tells you, 'that rod was making the Autobots see things that weren't there.'

'Good job you guys were here,' Bumblebee tells you, grinning.

Bulkhead bends to examine the deactivated gardening 'bot. 'Looks like he's had some upgrades recently – Decepticon circuits.'

'Megatron sent him to get his hands on the Allspark,' guesses Bumblebee, 'is it safe?'

Bulkhead looks back at the still smouldering building behind you. 'Maybe I'd better go and get it,' he suggests.

A few moments later he returns with his box. 'Wonder if this is one of the fakes?' he asks.

'Only one way to find out,' replies Bumblebee.

If the box contains the Allspark, turn to 10.

If it contains a fake, turn to 50.

A small crack appears at the point of impact. It begins to spider-web across the grey surface of the Dome and soon the whole thing is covered in thin jagged lines.

You reach out and prod the Dome with a single finger. Silently and rather beautifully the Dome collapses into dust.

'Hey, am I glad to see you guys,' rumbles the deep voice of Bulkhead.

'What happened to you?' asks Bumblebee.

The huge destruction 'bot shrugs his massive shoulders. 'I don't know,' he confesses, 'but I guess I had the real Allspark.' He indicates the box he is holding which is glowing slightly.

Suddenly from out of the darkness two more vehicles appear. They pull to a stop and change into 'bots.

'Ratchet and Prime!' squeals Sari.

Bumblebee looks at Bulkhead. 'Now you're in trouble,' he teases.

If Prime speaks, turn to 71.

If Ratchet speaks, turn to 101.

Sari suggests that you have a look for yourself. She unstraps her personal computer – a small unit about the size of a large watch that she wears on her wrist, presses a button and then passes it to you.

The tiny screen shows a slightly wonky picture of the hothead Autobot called Bumblebee.

'Optimus Prime has asked me to give you a message, Sari Sumdac,' says Bumblebee on the recorded message, 'Keep away from our base. It is not safe for you to visit us at present.'

You frown. 'That doesn't sound like the Bumblebee I see on the news feeds,' you say.

Sari is also frowning now. 'Now you come to mention it, that is a bit odd,' she agrees.

'It could be some kind of trick,' you say, 'to make you keep away?'

If Sari thinks you might be right, turn to 52.

If she disagrees, turn to 20.

59

You find yourself in a dark passageway and stop dead. Sari pushes you from behind.

'Just walk forward,' she tells you. 'There's another door in a bit.'

Your eyes are beginning to adapt to the dark now and you can just about see a metre or so in front of you. You are in a small inner lobby leading to another door. You open the door and step through into another dark corridor. This corridor is wider and Sari steps up to walk alongside you. The only source of light is the glow from Sari's Key.

'That's odd,' she comments, 'the lights would be on if someone was here.'

'So there's no-one at home?' you conclude.

Sari frowns. 'I guess so,' she agrees.

Suddenly you hear the sound of a motor engine nearby.

If Sari runs off towards the sound, turn to 29.

If you take more caution, turn to 97.

Bulkhead appears behind the stranger and calls out.

'Careful Bumblebee,' he warns, 'this guy is as tough as he looks!'

Bumblebee puts you and Sari down and zooms back towards the stranger.

'You big 'bots are all the same,' he proclaims, 'you think size is everything but it doesn't matter how massive you are if you're slower than a snail.'

Bumblebee runs in a tight circle round the stranger, who hits out with one massive arm but fails to find the speedster.

'I will crush you like a flea,' announces the stranger in a deep voice that makes the building shake.

'Got to catch me first,' replies Bumblebee, but then the stranger connects and Bumblebee sails through the air backwards.

'My name is Crush-A,' the stranger announces, 'I'm a clearance 'bot. And today I'm going to clear you.'

If Bumblebee replies, turn to 42.

If Bulkhead replies, turn to 85.

You run after Sari.

I'm sorry,' you tell her, 'I didn't mean to make you cry.'

Sari stops and wipes her eyes.

'It's not your fault, I'm just so worried,' she confesses.

She tells you that she hasn't seen the Autobots for days and you realise that you've not seen the robot superheroes on the news recently either.

'Maybe they're on a mission off planet,' you suggest.

'They wouldn't do that without leaving me a message,' Sari tells you.

'Have you looked for one at their base?' you ask. 'They may have left you a note.'

Sari grins. 'Why didn't I think of that?' she wonders out loud. 'Come on then, let's go and see if they left me anything.'

'Are you sure you want to take me with you?' you ask her.

If Sari insists you accompany, her turn to 11.

If Sari now hesitates, turn to 95.

The vehicle changes into a sleek robot shape. It is a bright yellow colour and you realise with relief that it is Bumblebee – the Autobot.

He points his arms at the cleaning robot and fires a blast of electrical energy at it. Immediately the suction tube drops you.

'Something's scrambled your circuits, pal,' he tells the cleaning robot, 'people might be messy but we don't put them in the trash!'

The cleaning robot makes a move towards Bumblebee, swinging the tube towards him. Bumblebee is too fast for it and dances out of the way.

'You suck!' he jokes and fires another blast at it. This time the machine comes to a juddering halt and the headlights go out.

Bumblebee comes over to you and makes sure you are okay.

If you were attacked on the street, turn to 17.

If you were attacked inside the factory, turn to 69.

63

Sari is watching Crush-A carefully. 'There's something strange about that 'bot,' she tells you, 'look at the way it moves.' When you take a second look you can see what Sari means: there's a little bit of stiffness to the action.

'He's like a remote control toy,' you realise.

Sari nods her head in agreement. 'Yeah that's it,' she shouts back at you, 'he's not an independent 'bot at all. Someone's controlling him.'

'Whoever it is would need to be close,' you suggest. You both start looking around for a suitable vantage point. You see a glass-walled room overlooking the area where the fight is happening. 'Up there!' you call over to Sari.

Bumblebee comes spinning towards you, hurled by Crush-A. When he gets to his feet you tell him about what you have seen. Bumblebee takes one look at the target and then roars off at top speed. Just moments later Crush-A suddenly freezes and topples over. Bumblebee reappears holding an angry looking man in a white coat. He has no hair and thick-lensed spectacles.

'Who are you?' demands Optimus Prime.

The stranger tries to stand tall which is difficult when Bumblebee is holding his arms behind him. 'I am Doctor Cornelius Lighthouse, the human genius that nearly unlocked the secrets of your precious Allspark,' he announces.

'Yeah well "nearly" is the key word, loser!' replies Bumblebee.

'Anyway,' adds Optimus Prime, 'there was never any real threat to the Allspark.'

'But you were scared enough to hide it?!' claims Lighthouse. 'I came so close to getting the Allspark for my research!'

'Not really,' grins Prime, 'all the boxes contained fakes.'

The police arrive and take Lighthouse away.

If you are in the Library, turn to 105.

If you are in the Night Club, turn to 103.

Prowl splits you into two teams. He and Bulkhead will approach the Library from the front while you, Sari and Bumblebee try and find an entrance point at the back of the building.

It's late now and the library is closed for the night. There are hardly any lights on inside the multistorey building.

'Look,' says Sari, pointing up near a fire escape. 'I think that window is open.' The window in question is very small but with Bumblebee's help you and Sari manage to squeeze through.

'There's no way I can get in there,' complains Bumblebee, 'not without scratching my paintwork!'

You promise to try and find a door to let him in.

You find a way to get into the main part of the Library where you suddenly come across a familiar figure.

If you met Crush-A earlier, turn to 19.

If you have not encountered Crush-A, turn to 27.

The energy blasts seems to disappear into the force-field which glows with a bright light and then appears to turn solid.

Prowl is not impressed. 'Now look what you've done!' he complains.

You tentatively tap at the suddenly solid dome and find that it makes a hollow sound.

'At least we can touch it now,' you point out.

Prowl frowns and checks out the wall for himself. He starts tapping the dome at different points, listening carefully to the sounds from within.

'What's he doing?' Sari asks.

Bumblebee shrugs. 'Search me! Maybe his circuits got scrambled earlier.'

Prowl fixes him with a cold look. 'I'm listening for a weak spot,' he explains, 'and I think I've found one.'

Prowl takes careful aim and then hits the dome with a slicing karate chop.

If the dome shatters, turn to 88.

If a small crack appears, turn to 57.

'You're right,' you tell Sari, 'You know the Autobots better than anyone. There's no way a fake Bumblebee could fool you.'

The Professor takes a step towards Bulkhead. 'The children are confused,' he tells the massive demolition 'bot, 'destroy the fake now!

Sari and you exchange looks. You have to stop Bulkhead somehow.

You see that the Professor is still operating the controls on his so-called scanner.

'That machine,' Sari hisses at you in a whisper, 'I'm sure that is the key.'

You nod and start running towards the Professor.

'Get back,' he cries out but you ignore him and jump towards him, reaching out for the equipment hanging around his neck. You yank at the strap and it breaks, releasing the machine into your possession.

'Bumblebee, blast it!' shouts Sari

If Bumblebee manages to fire at the machine, turn to 40.

If Bulkhead gets in the way, turn to 14.

The stranger starts to speak. His deep voice echoes off the buildings around you.

'I am Crush-A,' he tells you, 'Site Clearance Specialist and if you do not back off I will clear you!'

'He's got the Allspark,' whispers Sari to Bumblebee, pointing at the box that Crush-A is holding.

'Let's hope it's not the real one,' Bumblebee replies, reminding you that each of the Autobots took a box like this to hide and that only one of them had the genuine Allspark.

Bumblebee leaves you and Sari at a safe distance and moves closer.

'You've got something there that doesn't belong to you,' he tells him.

Crush-A bounces the box in his hand, like a kid with a ball.

'What are you going to do about it?' he asks.

Behind him you see Bulkhead appear in a doorway.

If Bumblebee answers, turn to 42.

If Bulkhead answers, turn to 85.

68

You turn around and begin to run but you realise that all these streets look the same and you soon find that you are totally lost.

You have no idea which direction to go.

It seems to have become much darker.

You are beginning to get a little bit scared.

Suddenly someone grabs your shoulder from behind.

'Where did you get to?' asks a familiar voice. It is Sari. 'You should stick close to me,' she advises, 'you don't want to get lost in this neighbourhood.'

You bite your tongue and stop yourself from pointing out that it wasn't you who disappeared but Sari is already heading off again, at her usual fast pace.

You feel a shudder as if someone is watching you and glance over your shoulder.

If you think you can see a vehicle parked in the street, turn to 48.

If you think you can see a man, turn to 12.

Bumblebee makes sure that the cleaning robot had been totally deactivated. There are still blue sparks of energy running around its body. He pulls out a small circuit board from the central processor.

'This is why the machine attacked you,' he tells you.

'What is it?' asks Sari.

'An override control circuit,' Bumblebee answers her. 'Prowl got word that Megatron had found a way to install these in a whole range of City Authority 'Bots and was about to launch a major attack on us.'

'So where are the other Autobots now?' you ask, fearing the worst. Bumblebee shrugs. 'I don't know,' he confesses. 'This wasn't the plan.'

'What was the plan?' Sari asks.

Bumblebee sits down on one of the giant Autobot-sized sofas and explains. Optimus Prime decided that the most important thing was to defend the Allspark, the mystical source of all robot life. If that was to fall into Megatron's control then he would become all powerful. To avoid that the Autobots came up with a plan to hide the Allspark in order to protect it. They placed the Allspark in one of five identical boxes and put fakes in the other four.

'Then we picked a box at random and set off to hide them somewhere,' Bumblebee tells you.

'So no-one knew which of you had the real Allspark?' you realise.

Bumblebee nods. 'Yeah, great plan, huh? Trouble is we were all meant to meet back here but looks like I'm the only one who made it.'

'So what happened to the others?' Sari asks. Bumblebee doesn't have an answer.

'Then we have to find them,' you tell the others.

'But how?' asks Bumblebee. Suddenly the view screen crackles into life, and an Autobot appears.

If it is Ratchet, turn to 80.

If it is Prowl, turn to 30.

Optimus Prime stands at the open doorway.

'Quick!' he calls to Bumblebee, 'We need your help.'

He turns and runs back into the main auditorium. Bumblebee hurries to follow him. You and Sari go too.

Inside the club there is total pandemonium. A massive enemy 'bot is engaged in battle with the Autobots and he appears to be holding his own.

'I am Crush-A.' declares the enemy, throwing both Prowl and Bumblebee aside with ease, 'and I will claim the Allspark for Megatron and the Deceptions!' he continues.

Ratchet is also there and he launches an attack on the enemy 'bot but gets upended by Crush-A.

Sari grabs you by the hand. 'We need to help them,' she tells you.

'What can we do?' you ask her.

Sari shrugs. 'There must be something here.'

If you have an idea, turn to 44.

If Sari has an idea, turn to 63.

'Well done Autobots, the danger is over,' announces Prime.

'It is?' says Bumblebee hopefully.

'Looks that way,' adds Ratchet, 'I've deadlocked our base systems to keep Megatron and his agents out, so the Allspark will be safe there again now.'

Optimus Prime takes the box from Bulkhead's hands. 'And we now know that the Allspark can protect itself too. What were you thinking when the force-field activated, Bulkhead?'

'Nothing!' replies Bulkhead.

'No change there, then!' jokes Bumblebee.

'No I mean nothing except that I had to protect the Allspark,' explains Bulkhead.

Prime nods. 'You see the Allspark read your mind and provided its own protection.'

Sari introduces you to Optimus Prime and Ratchet.

'Thank you,' Optimus Prime tells you seriously, 'we appreciate your help. But now it's time to get you home, I think.'

'I'll give you a ride,' offers Bumblebee and changes. 'Let's roll out...'

YOUR ADVENTURE WITH THE TRANSFORMERS IS OVER

Without warning, a massive window above the main entrance to the Gallery is smashed by something within, sending shards of broken glass showering down on to the street. Luckily Bumblebee's incredible speed enables him to whisk you and Sari out of danger before the glass gets anywhere near you.

You can see a massive robot-shape in the ragged hole where the window used to be.

'Is that Bulkhead up there?' you ask Sari.

'It's hard to see from this angle,' she tells you.

The robot in question suddenly jumps down from the broken window, landing heavily on the sidewalk and cracking the paving stones with his weight. It is a massive robot with huge arms but it is not Bulkhead.

You see that the strange robot is holding a box.

If the strange robot speaks to you, turn to 67.

If Bulkhead appears behind the robot, turn to 60.

73

It is a human that is speaking. A man, with wild grey hair and thick-lensed glasses. He speaks with a slight European accent.

'My name is Professor Heinz Von Furstwartz, and I am an expert in robotics from the University of Vienna,' he explains.

Out of the corner of your eye you see that Bumblebee is beginning to recover.

'What makes you think Bumblebee's a fake, then?' you challenge the Professor.

'This tells me,' he says and indicates a machine that he is wearing around his neck. It looks a bit like a giant remote control. You can see that it has lights and dials on it. 'It scans and analyses machines and robots and gives a read-out showing the origins of all components.'

If you ask for a demonstration from the Professor, turn to 36.

If Bulkhead attacks Bumblebee again, turn to 79.

It's a long trip on the subway out into one of the big industrial parts of old Detroit. Sari makes you promise never to reveal the location of the Autobots' base.

'There was this whole abandoned auto plant,' she tells you. 'My Dad owns it, but has forgotten all about it.'

You get out at the subway stop and make your way through the dark and quiet streets. In the distance you can see the bright lights and tall buildings of modern Detroit but here lots of buildings are boarded up and the higher windows are full of broken frames of glass.

There is no-one else around but suddenly you see a flash of movement out of the corner of your eye. You spin round but there's nothing there.

'Did you see that?' you ask Sari.

If she did, turn to 87.

If she didn't, turn to 98.

75

Sari disappears into the darkness and for a moment there is silence. Has something happened to her? You hesitate, not sure if you dare follow.

'Come on then,' Sari calls from beyond the door, 'Just be careful – the lights are out.'

Feeling a little foolish you step through the doorway into a dark corridor.

Your eyes begin to adjust to the lack of light and you can make out Sari a few metres down the passageway.

'The living area is down here,' she tells you. 'This is weird though, the lights should come on when anyone is here.'

You shrug. 'So that just tells us that no-one is here,' you point out.

'That's why it's weird though,' Sari replies, 'we're here, aren't we?'

Somewhere nearby you hear movement and an engine.

If Sari runs off towards the sound, turn to 29.

If you are more cautious, turn to 97.

'I know that one,' you exclaim.

Bulkhead scratches his head. 'Go on then – when is a door not a door?'

'When it's ajar!' you say.

Bulkhead shakes his head. 'I still don't get it.'

'When something is ajar,' you explain, 'it means it is just slightly open. It's a sort of pun; a play on words. The word "ajar" sound just like "a jar" – something you keep jam in.'

'So we have to find a jam factory?' asks Bulkhead

Sari laughs. 'It's not about a jam factory,' she interjects, 'it must be about the Jam Jar. It's a old warehouse that's now a music club where anyone can join in with the band on stage.'

You look at her in surprise.

'They do kid's shows on Saturday mornings,' she explains.

If you all go to the Jam Jar, turn to 84.

If you split up, turn to 35.

Prowl is standing there.

'We need you - now,' Prowl states and disappears back into the auditorium.

Bumblebee runs after him.

You and Sari exchange looks – should you go too?

'Come on,' says Sari and grabs you by the hand. She leads you into the main part of the club where you discover a mighty battle going on. A huge clearance 'bot is fighting all of the Autobots – Ratchet, Prowl, Prime, Bulkhead and Bumblebee and, to your surprise, the enemy is winning!

'I am Crush-A and I will crush you all,' screams the enemy 'bot. 'Where is the Allspark?'

You see that the enemy 'bot has Optimus Prime pinned down under one massive hand.

'We have to help them somehow,' whispers Sari to you.

You look around you – what can you do?

If you have an idea, turn to 44.

If Sari has an idea, turn to 63.

A trilling sound comes from Sari's pocket. It's her personal communicator. She opens it up and tells you that it's a message from Optimus Prime.

'He says he's with Ratchet and they need back up,' she tells you.

'Where are they?' asks Bulkhead.

'He doesn't want to say on an open channel.'

'So how are we going to find him?' demands Bumblebee, 'It could take forever to look for him, even at my speed.'

'Relax,' replies Sari, 'he's given us a clue so we can work out where to go.'

'What is the clue?' you ask.

Sari tells you that Optimus Prime has sent you a riddle as a clue.

'What's black and white and read all over?' she reads out.

For a moment there is silence while you all think about it.

If you have an idea, turn to 93.

If Sari has the answer, turn to 34.

Bulkhead suddenly leaps forward, arms pumping, ready for action.

'Enough talking,' he roars, 'that impostor needs taking down.'

Bravely, Sari runs out in front of him. 'Wait,' she screams and, to your relief, Bulkhead stops dead.

'Maybe the Professor's machine made a mistake,' she says.

The Professor shakes his head. 'My scans shows that this 'bot was made in Detroit not outer space,' he tells you.

Sari shakes her head. 'No, you're wrong, I know you are.'

You look between Sari and the Professor. Both seem so absolutely convinced by their arguments. You realise that they can't both be right.

You see that Bumblebee is beginning to get to his feet. Bulkhead flexes his huge pile-driver fists. The Professor's machine is still active, dials and read-outs flashing.

You have to make a decision.

If you decide to believe Sari, turn to 66.

If you decide to believe the Professor, turn to 18.

The screen clears and you can see that the Autobot at the other end of the two-way communications link is Ratchet. He does not look happy.

'Bumblebee – are you the only one back?' he asks.

Bumblebee nods. Ratchet makes a noise that sounds a bit like a growl.

'Something has gone wrong,' he tells you. 'Megatron and his agents must have discovered our plan.'

'Did you hide your box safely?' Bumblebee asks.

Ratchet shakes his head sharply once. 'Negative. I was attacked as soon as I arrived here in Paris.'

'Are you okay?' Sari asks in a concerned tone.

Ratchet lowers his eyes, almost as if he was embarrassed.

'I'm still standing,' he says, 'the other guy isn't.'

Ratchet tells you to find Bulkhead.

If Ratchet tells you to go to New York, turn to 55.

If Ratchet tells you to go to Los Angeles, turn to 3.

Sari shakes her head. 'It might be dangerous,' she tells you. 'Perhaps it will be safer if you stay here.'

'And let you go alone?' you point out. 'Is that a good idea?'

Sari reconsiders and then nods. 'Come on then.'

She takes you on a subway ride to one of the older parts of the City. You've not been in this area of Detroit before; these days very few people have.

'This is where all the car factories used to be,' Sari explains, 'back in the twentieth century.'

You look around you at all the boarded-up factories. It's hard to imagine these derelict buildings in their heyday, producing thousands of cars daily.

'It's like a sort of ghost town,' you comment but Sari doesn't answer. You realise that you cannot see her.

If you call out her name, turn to 7.

If you turn around, turn to 68.

Bumblebee's energy blasts ricochet off the Dome's wall and head back towards the spot where you and Sari are standing. Prowl moves quickly and pulls the pair of you clear of danger.

'That wasn't very smart,' he tells Bumblebee.

Bumblebee looks embarrassed, 'Sorry,' he apologises, 'my bad!'

'At least we can see and touch it now,' you point out. The force-field is now a solid grey wall in the shape of a tall dome. You tap on the wall and it sounds hollow. Prowl comes across to join you. He starts patting the curved wall at different points and listening intently

'I think that flight through the air scrambled his circuits,' whispers Bumblebee.

'Your blasts weakened it,' Prowl explains; 'now I will finish the job.'

He kicks out at a precise spot on the wall.

If the dome shatters, turn to 88.

If a small crack appears, turn to 57.

83

You suggest to Bumblebee that he looks for the other Autobots by thinking about where they might have gone to hide their boxes.

‘If you’re going to hide something like that you are probably going to use a hiding place somewhere you know,’ you continue.

Bumblebee thinks you might be on to something. ‘That makes sense,’ he tells you, ‘I went to my favourite place – the Race Track - to hide mine.’

Sari is also nodding in agreement. ‘So where do we think Bulkhead would go?’ she asks, ‘what are his favourite places in the city?’

Bumblebee thinks for a moment. ‘The City Art Gallery,’ he announces. ‘Bulkhead spends hours there looking at the different paintings.’

‘But he also visits the Detroit Sculpture Park,’ adds Sari.

If you decide to go to the Art Gallery, turn to 102.

If you decide to go to the Sculpture Park, turn to 45.

You all hurry back to downtown Detroit to the club.

When you arrive you find it has been closed for refurbishment. But the front door appears to be unlocked. Prowl suggests that you should wait.

'We need a strategy,' he suggests. 'We don't know what we might find in there.'

'What do you want us to do?' asks Bumblebee, 'sit out here and hope Prime comes out eventually?'

Prowl shakes his head. 'We go in two waves. Bulkhead and I will find a rear entrance while you take the front. Remember Prime called for back up so be prepared for trouble!'

Prowl and Bulkhead disappear round the side of the building.

When Bumblebee leads you into the club, you hear the sound of battle nearby. Suddenly a pair of doors burst open.

If you met Crush-A earlier, turn to 77.

If you have not encountered Crush-A, turn to 70.

'We're going to stop you of course,' rumbles Bulkhead and hits the ground with his pile-driver arms but Crush-A manages to remain upright.

'Is that your best shot?' he taunts and swings one of his arms in an arc, knocking Bulkhead off his feet.

Bumblebee hurries to join the fight. He zaps the enemy 'bot with multiple energy blasts. Crush-A is distracted but not damaged by the attack. He grabs hold of a lamppost, rips it out of the ground and swings at Bumblebee. The speedster Autobot leaps in the air as the lamppost bat swings dangerously through the air. The lamppost imbeds itself in a wall sending a shockwave back into Crush-A, who is forced to drop his makeshift weapon.

'He's strong but he's not that smart,' Bumblebee shouts to Bulkhead.

'Sounds familiar,' says Bulkhead.

'Ah, you're not so dumb,' says Bumblebee, as he buzzes around Crush-A, zapping him with more tiny energy blasts. You can see that this is beginning to really annoy Crush-A. Distracted by Bumblebee, he doesn't see Bulkhead creeping a little bit closer.

'Now!' shouts Bulkhead and Bumblebee stops his attack and pulls away. For a moment Crush-A stands there looking dazed and dizzy and then Bulkhead clobbers him with his demolition ball. The clearance robot hits the deck with a loud thump.

Bulkhead checks his box. 'Looks like the real Allspark is still out there,' he announces, 'this is one of the fakes.'

Crush-A disappears in a flash of blue light.

A new figure appears in the doorway. It is the Autobot called Prowl.

'I heard you might need me,' he says.

'You're too late,' replies Bumblebee, 'you missed all the fun.'

If you get a message from Ratchet, turn to 100.

If you get a message from Prime, turn to 78.

Bumblebee leads the way through the broken gates.

It is very dark inside the park and rather scary. As you walk through, different works of art loom out of the gloom. A giant statue of an ape made out of shopping trolleys appears to reach down towards you but it is just an illusion.

Suddenly you see something moving ahead of you.

Bumblebee puts out an arm to stop you walking any further.

'Wait here,' he tells you.

He moves forward with uncharacteristic caution.

You grab Sari's hand and give it a squeeze.

The darkness envelopes Bumblebee completely.

For a moment it is as quiet as a grave and then suddenly something is moving through the air towards you, crashing through branches of a tree.

A robot figure falls at your feet

If it is Bumblebee, turn to 104.

If it is not Bumblebee, turn to 23.

'It was just that,' Sari tells you, pointing back down the street. You see a robot street cleaner, moving so slowly that you ignored it before. It has a huge vacuum pipe on a robot arm which is sucking up dirt and rubbish from the sidewalk.

You frown. Whatever it was you saw out of the corner of your eye was moving faster than that, wasn't it?

'Come on,' Sari insists, holding the Key she wears around her neck, 'this is vibrating like crazy - which must mean we're close.'

'Close to what?' you ask.

Sari grins. 'To an Autobot,' she replies and then adds, 'or a Decepticon, of course!'

You look behind you and notice that the street cleaner is now much closer to you. Suddenly the vacuum pipe swings towards you.

If you are sucked towards the machine, turn to 15.

If you turn and run, turn to 37.

88

The Dome shatters into thousands of tiny pieces, revealing Bulkhead inside. He is holding his Allspark box which is glowing with a bright light. The Key around Sari's neck begins to glow with a similar light and then all the broken fragments of the Dome float into the air and disappear into the Allspark. The light turns itself off and all is quiet and dark once more. Prowl changes into his vehicle form and shines his headlamps on you all, so you can see each other.

You can hear the sound of other engines approaching.

'Decepticons?' you wonder.

Bulkhead and Bumblebee take up a defensive position with you, Sari and the Allspark box between them. Prowl circles round to point his lamps towards the approaching vehicles.

Two vehicles pull up and change. To your relief you see that it is Ratchet and Optimus Prime.

If Prime speaks, turn to 71.

If Ratchet speaks, turn to 101.

'It was weird,' Sari explains to you, 'I just got this email from them telling me to keep away.'

'And they didn't give you a reason?' you ask, intrigued by the uncharacteristic behaviour of the Autobots.

'No, nothing,' says Sari shaking her head. 'It's been almost a week now, and I've not seen any of them.'

You cast your mind back over the last few days. You don't pay a lot of attention to the newscasts but you are always interested to see reports about the Autobots. Recently though, there has been nothing about them in the news. Thinking back you realise that no-one seems to have seen any of the Autobots for a week.

'Do you think something might have happened to them?' you wonder. 'Perhaps that message was a fake!'

If Sari thinks you might be right, turn to 52.

If she disagrees, turn to 20.

90

The force-field becomes visible for a brief moment and you can see that it is a dirty grey dome about the size of a small house. The curved sides are too steep to climb. You run around the outside and realise that it is a perfect circle. The circumference - the distance around the edge of the circle - is about fifty paces. Suddenly the grey surface fizzles and it disappears again.

Sari is disappointed that her Key did not get you inside the force-field.

'Sorry guys,' she said, 'it didn't work.'

'At least we got a glimpse of what we're dealing with,' says Bumblebee.

Prowl has his head close to the force-field, listening.

'I think Bulkhead is in there,' he announces.

'Stand back,' orders Bumblebee and fires off a huge energy blast.

If the blasts just bounce off the dome, turn to 82.

If the dome absorbs the energy, turn to 65.

Sari tells you that she thinks she knows the answer. 'So what is it?' asks Bulkhead.

'Listen carefully,' Sari tells him, 'when is a door not a door? When it's ajar.'

Bulkhead, Bumblebee and Prowl just look at her.

'I get it,' you tell Sari. 'You see when something is ajar,' you explain to the Autobots, 'it means it is just slightly open.'

'But what does it mean?' asks Bulkhead

Sari clicks her fingers. 'We need to get back to Downtown Detroit,' she exclaims. 'They must be at the Jam Jar Club - where anyone can join in with the group that are playing. I went to one of their kids' Saturday morning shows once. It's a great place. Used to be an old warehouse now it's a hang out for musicians.'

If you all go to the Jam Jar, turn to 84.

If you split up, turn to 35.

As Bumblebee drives through the city you and Sari try to think of a plan. Suddenly Sari has an idea.

'Where did you go to hide your box?' she asks.

'The Race Track,' replies Bumblebee.

'Why there?' you ask.

Bumblebee tells you that he needed to choose somewhere he knew well enough to find a good hiding place.

'That's it,' announces Sari, 'If we can just work out where the other Autobots went to hide their boxes we might be able to find them.'

'What about Bulkhead?' you ask, 'where does he like to go in the City?'

'He likes looking at the paintings at the City Art Gallery,' Bumblebee tells you, 'and he also likes to spend time at the Detroit Sculpture Park.'

If you decide to go to the Art Gallery, turn to 102.

If you decide to go to the Sculpture Park, turn to 45.

'I think I know what it is,' you announce. Everyone turns to look at you expectantly.

'Go on,' says Sari, 'tell us.'

'Well it's a book, isn't it? Black and white – that's the printing, the words on the paper and it's read all over, because people read books everywhere, don't they?'

'I thought it meant the colour red,' says Bumblebee.

'But what kind of clue is that – a book? There must be loads of bookshops in the city,' says Sari.

'But there's only one Central Library isn't there?' you point out, 'and it's huge.'

Bumblebee wants to speed to the Library straight away but Prowl thinks you should be more cautious. 'Prime wants us to provide backup,' he reminds you, 'not run into more trouble.'

'And don't forget that Crush-A guy is out there somewhere, too,' says Bulkhead.

If Prowl suggests a strategy, turn to 64.

If you go directly to the Library, turn to 28.

Sari takes you to the nearest subway station and before you know it you are climbing the steps out of a station down in the old industrial neighbourhood.

It is as if you have travelled back in time to the middle of the twentieth century when Detroit was at the heart of the American car industry. You look around you at the massive buildings and wonder what it must have been like when these huge sites were producing thousands of cars every month.

Of course these days they look a bit different. These dark and lifeless buildings haven't been used for years; many of the windows are broken or boarded-up.

'Why would the Autobots want to live out here?' you wonder.

Sari doesn't answer. You realise that she has vanished.

If you call out her name, turn to 7.

If you turn around, turn to 68.

Sari hesitates and looks for a moment as if she has changed her mind.

'It might be dangerous...' she begins.

'In that case, it would be safer if someone came with you,' you suggest.

Sari nods in agreement.

She tells you that the Autobots have a secret base in an old car factory that her father owns.

'He's got bits and pieces of property all over Detroit,' she tells you, 'but he often forgets about them.'

The Autobots' base is in a district where a lot of car manufacturing used to happen back in the twentieth century, when Detroit was known as Motor City. The site looks uninhabited but Sari assures you that this is the right place.

She leads you to a small side door. 'After you,' she says opening the door.

If you go in first, turn to 59.

If you want Sari to go first, turn to 75.

96

Sari screams and drops the Key. 'It got all hot,' she explains.

'That didn't work then,' says Bumblebee.

'There must be some way to get inside,' insists Prowl.

'Or to get what is inside out,' you add. 'If Bulkhead is in there, perhaps there is something he can do to help.'

Bumblebee nods and goes to stand as close as he dares to the invisible force-field.

'Hey, Bulkhead!' he calls out, 'Can you hear me?'

You and Sari hold your breath as you wait but there is no answer.

Prowl shakes his head. 'The force-field must keep everything out,' he concludes, 'including sound waves.'

Bumblebee is beginning to lose his patience and before Prowl can stop him he extends his arms and hurls an energy blast into the force-field.

If the blasts just bounce off, turn to 82.

If the force-field absorbs the energy, turn to 65.

Sari's face lights up. 'Autobots,' she says.

'Or the other lot,' you remind her. 'It could be one of their enemies, the Decepticons.'

Sari stops herself and nods. 'Good point,' she tells you. 'Ratchet is always telling us not to jump to conclusions.'

'Isn't Ratchet a bit scary?' you ask Sari.

She grins. 'He's a bit fierce but okay when you get to know him,' she whispers. 'Now, we need to make like Prowl...'

Walking carefully she leads you into the main living area of the Autobots. The engine noise is louder here.

She indicates for you to go one way and she goes the other. You separate to encircle whatever it is. As you get closer you begin to wish that you had stayed together.

Suddenly something moves towards you out of the darkness.

If it is Sari, turn to 41.

If it is a robot, turn to 31.

Sari shakes her head, a puzzled expression on her face.

'No, nothing,' she assures you.

Without warning, the strange Key that Sari wears around her neck begins to glow.

'What's that?' you ask.

Sari frowns. 'It's kinda hard to explain,' she tells you, 'it's a Key that's connected to the Autobots and their enemies the Decepticons too.'

'So what does it mean, when it glows like that?'

'I don't really know,' Sari confesses. 'It might mean one of them is nearby.'

'An Autobot!' you gasp, looking around.

'Or a Decepticon,' Sari reminds you.

You see a slow-moving vehicle coming along the street. It's a street-cleaner with a massive vacuum pipe to clear rubbish from the roadside.

As it comes closer the robot arm controlling the vacuum pipe suddenly swings round towards you.

If you are sucked towards the machine, turn to 15.

If you turn and run, turn to 37.

The main doors of the Art Gallery are blown off their hinges and come flying out towards you. Bumblebee grabs you and Sari in his arms and whisks you out of the way.

There is a great deal of smoke in the gaping hole where the doors used to be and then a shadowy figure begins to emerge.

'Bulkhead!' shouts Sari in delight, but to your horror the figure that steps out into the night air is not the destruction 'bot but another robot entirely.

It is a similar size to Bulkhead, with big powerful arms and a squat sturdy body. It does not have legs but rolls on giant caterpillar tracks like a tank. In one of its massive hands it is holding a box.

If the strange robot speaks to you, turn to 67.

If Bulkhead appears behind the robot, turn to 60.

100

Something starts vibrating in Sari's jacket pocket.

'Is that your Key going all weird again?' you ask her.

She shakes her head. 'It's my phone,' she tells you pulling out the tiny communications device. It is Ratchet calling.

'Autobots Prime and I need your assistance urgently,' he says, his voice coming out of the tiny speaker with amazing clarity.

'We'll be right there,' Bumblebee tells him, 'just as soon as you tell us where to go.'

'Negative on that,' says Ratchet, 'this is not a secure line. Other ears might be listening.'

'So how do we find you?' asks Prowl.

'Answer this riddle and you'll soon find us,' Ratchet says 'When is a door not a door?'

Ratchet reminds you to be quick and ends the call. You all try to solve his riddle.

If you have an idea, turn to 76.

If Sari has the answer, turn to 91.

'Autobots, stand down, the danger is over,' barks Ratchet, as if giving orders in battle.

Sari introduces you to Ratchet and Prime and explains how you've been helping with the quest.

'Is it really safe to go back to your base – what about Megatron?' you ask.

'I've fixed up the security – there's no way Megatron or one of his agents can get in now,' Ratchet assures you.

'And anyway we now know that the Allspark can protect itself,' adds Optimus Prime. 'What were you thinking when the force-field activated Bulkhead?'

'Just that I had to protect the Allspark,' rumbles the big destruction 'bot.

Prime explains that the Allspark must have read Bulkhead's mind and produced the force-field shield. 'Okay Autobots, transform and roll out,' he announces.

Bumblebee comes over to you and Sari. 'Jump in,' he says, 'I'll get you home in style...'

YOUR ADVENTURE WITH THE TRANSFORMERS IS OVER

The Art Gallery is housed in an old mansion in downtown Detroit. It used to be a private house owned by a rich local businessman but these days it is home to a collection of paintings by famous artists from all over the world. The mansion itself has been extended with two new wings, one dedicated to artwork from comics and one dedicated to films.

Bumblebee pulls up outside the Gallery and lets you and Sari climb out before changing into his robot form.

'Oh boy, is this the dullest place in the city or what?' he asks looking at the imposing building in front of you.

Suddenly an alarm begins to sound and emergency lights come on in some of the rooms.

'Doesn't sound very dull now!' comments Sari.

If the main doors are knocked out, turn to 99.

If something smashes through a window, turn to 72.

'So where was the real Allspark?' you wonder.

'Safe where it always is,' Prime tells you.

'The decoys were just a way to force some of our enemies to show their hands,' adds Ratchet, 'and it worked perfectly,'

'But I have to thank you two,' Optimus Prime tells you and Sari, 'your bravery and assistance were invaluable tonight.'

You try not to blush but can't.

'Hey, why are you changing your paint job?' asks Bumblebee, as your face turns a bright shade of red.

Ratchet rumbles forward. 'I think it's time these young people got home to their beds,' he suggests and then glances over at Bumblebee, 'and there's some young Autobots who could do with a recharge too,' he adds.

Bumblebee changes into his vehicle form.

'Well, you may as well ride home in style,' he says, 'hop in.'

YOUR ADVENTURE WITH THE TRASNFORMERS IS OVER.

Bumblebee is lying in a crumpled heap in front of you but to your relief he gets to his feet, rubbing his head with a hand.

'Wow!' he exclaims, 'that was some ride!'

'What happened?' Sari asks.

'I ran into some kind of force-field,' replies Bumblebee. 'It was totally invisible and I just bounced off it.'

'But why would there be a force-field in a place like this?' you wonder.

'Good question,' says a new voice.

You whirl around and see that another 'bot has appeared from the darkness.

'Prowl!' exclaims Bumblebee, 'Do you have to sneak up like that. My circuits are jangling already!'

'Then you should find a moment to calm down,' Prowl says, 'I recommend meditation.'

If you suggest trying to find out how big the force-field is, turn to 13.

If you decide to try and find Bulkhead, turn to 5.

You step out from the library to find that it is a clear cold night and that the sky is full of stars.

Optimus Prime comes over to where you and Sari are standing.

'Thank you for all your help,' he tells you both, 'you were very brave.'

'There's just one thing I don't understand,' you confess, 'why did you hide a bunch of fake Allsparks?

'They were decoys,' explains Optimus Prime, 'It was a test, to make our enemies reveal themselves, and it worked.'

'And these two were more than brave,' says Bumblebee, 'it was like they were really part of the team.'

'Nevertheless, these humans have homes to go to,' adds Prime.

'Allow me to run you guys home,' says Bumblebee, taking the hint, 'I mean why go cargo when you can travel first class!'

'Transform and roll out,' orders Optimus Prime.

YOUR ADVENTURE WITH THE TRANSFORMERS IS OVER.